Great Eagle
AND SMALL ONE

by Ralph Moisa Jr.

Perfection Learning® CA

Cover Photo: Curt Stahr
Inside Illustration: Randy Messer

About the Author

Ralph Moisa Jr., a descendant of the Yaqui Nation, has spent many years researching the history and customs of many tribes, including his own. For over 20 years, he has performed and presented Indian history across the United States. He strives to help all people see the Indian world through an Indian's eyes.

Mr. Moisa also serves the Indian community and speaks in support of Indian causes. Using his own experiences, he warns against the dangers of prejudice and emphasizes the numerous benefits of a diverse society. In this way, he hopes to help people understand and appreciate all races.

Mr. Moisa currently resides in upstate New York with his wife, Carol, and his children, Bryan and Alicia.

> *"I have to do something for the creatures of this world and for this planet. I can't just be there. I have to make a difference."*

Ralph Moisa III

9/16/76   12/05/95

This book, this story, is dedicated to our son, who was electrocuted while trying to rescue a red-tailed hawk trapped on top of a utility pole. The first thoughts of this lesson started with him and the ring I gave him.

The lesson grew through the years as he grew and now is shared with you.

It is our hope that this story will leave an impression on you. An impression similar to the one our son left with those who knew and loved him.

In his memory, we will honor his sacrifice by giving 10 percent of our earnings from this book to programs that care for our winged friends. To people who care for the wounded and disabled birds of prey. This way their very important work will continue and the memory of our son will live on.

I thank you.
Ralph Moisa Jr.

Contents

Introduction 9

Chapter 1 11
Chapter 2 17
Chapter 3 25
Chapter 4 29
Chapter 5 37
Final Word 41
Chapter 6 42
Chapter 7 50

8

Listen, my friends. I want to tell you a story about Great Eagle. It was a long time ago. It was long before the Two-Leggeds walked this earth.

10

Chapter 1

The Creator spoke to Mother Earth. "I am proud of all living things. The rocks, the plants, and the fish. The animals and the birds are beautiful.

Even the crawling creatures have beauty. I respect them all. They are my creations. And they are perfect."

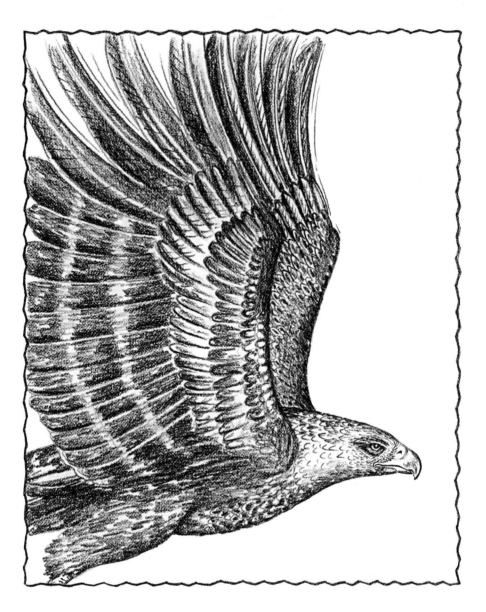

The Creator watched his creations.
And he was pleased.

One day, the Creator saw an eagle.
Great Eagle was his name.

Great Eagle cleaned his feathers for
hours. He combed them with his beak.
He stood straight on his branch. He
soared with the wind.

Great Eagle helped others. He was kind and gentle.

He hunted. But he took only what he needed. He did nothing wrong.

Great Eagle looked perfect. And all the creatures thought he was.

Chapter 2

Only the Creator could see deep into
Great Eagle's heart and deep into his
soul. And the Creator knew something
was missing. And He knew what it was.

"I love Great Eagle," the Creator said.
"So I must help him find what he is
missing. I want to help him be perfect."

So the Creator picked up a lightning
bolt. He threw it at Great Eagle. It took
away his left foot.

Great Eagle shouted in pain. "Why do you hurt me? Why are you so unfair?"

The Creator could not answer. How could He explain?

All Great Eagle could do was lie there.
He waited for the pain to stop. He waited
a long time.

Great Eagle grew hungry. But how
could he hunt?

He tried to stand. He fell over. He tried again. He fell again.

After many tries, Great Eagle stood. But he did not stand straight like before. His body was bent. It was hard to balance on only one foot.

Next, he tried to fly. But he couldn't.

Great Eagle looked at his wings.
Some of his feathers were broken.
Others were missing. How would he soar
on the wind like before?

He flapped his wings. But he didn't
rise. He just fell over.

So he flapped his wings again. Again
and again he tried. At last, he stayed
standing. He didn't fall.

He flapped his wings harder and
harder. Finally, he started to rise. Great
Eagle flew.

Chapter 3

Below him, he saw a rabbit hiding in a meadow.

Great Eagle had caught many rabbits before. "This will be easy," he thought.

He dove toward the rabbit. He opened his claws. He closed his claws on the rabbit and started to rise.

Something caught his eye. It was the rabbit running away. It was the very one he hunted.

What happened? How could he have dropped it? This had never happened before.

But he had always hunted with two good feet. That was when he was perfect.

What could he do now? How could he hunt? He would starve.

Great Eagle was weak from trying to stand. His wings hurt. He was too tired to go on. He flew back to his nest to give up.

Chapter 4

Great Eagle had many friends. And they saw what had happened. So they came to help.

But Great Eagle wasn't kind to them. He was still mad at the Creator. Why weren't his friends hurt the way he was? "Go away! I don't want your help," he shouted.

His friends were sad. They all flew away, all except one small eagle. His name was Small One.

Long ago, Great Eagle had been a special friend to Small One. And Small One had not forgotten.

You see, Small One's parents had been killed many years before. He had been left with no one to care for him.

He had been too young to care for himself. He would have died. But Great Eagle had watched over him.

Great Eagle had hunted for food for Small One. He had kept him warm. He had kept him safe.

Until one day, Small One was able to care for himself. Great Eagle knew it was time to say good-bye. He sent Small One off to build his own nest.

That was many years ago. But Small
One had never forgotten Great Eagle's
kindness. It made Small One sad to see
his friend hurting.

Small One loved Great Eagle. He
would not let Great Eagle send him
away.

Small One left to catch a fish. He
brought it back. He lay the fish beside
the great bird.

Great Eagle started to turn away. But
he was too hungry. He bit into the fish.
But he could not get a piece to come
loose.

Great Eagle had to lie on his back. He used his one good foot to pull at the fish. It was hard, and it was slow. But he was able to eat.

Small One brought him more fish. And he did not laugh at the way Great Eagle was eating.

At last, Great Eagle was full. He fell asleep.

36

Chapter 5

After some time, Great Eagle awoke.
He saw Small One sleeping beside him.

"I will try to fly again," he thought.
Then he remembered his broken
feathers. But that wasn't important to
him now.

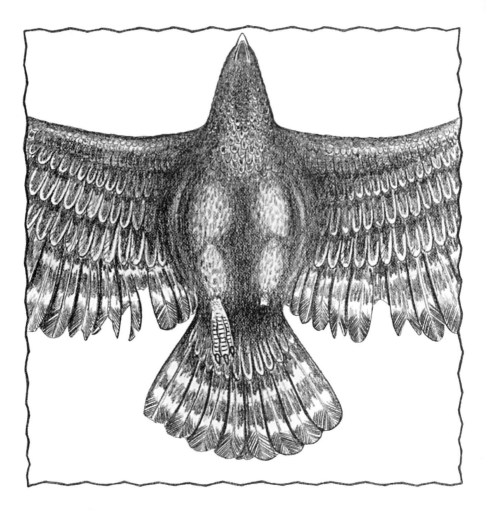

Great Eagle didn't care about combing his feathers. He did not work for hours like he had before. He had more important things to think about.

Great Eagle soared on the winds as he hunted. He dove, trying to catch his food. But he missed again and again.

Still he did not give up. He remembered Small One's kindness. This gave him the strength to keep trying.

As the days went by, Great Eagle became stronger. He learned to hunt with one foot. He felt proud.

Now he no longer needed Small One's help. Still, the two eagles stayed friends. They soared on the winds together.

The Creator looked down. And he smiled. "Now these two eagles are perfect," he said. "Not in how they look. But in their spirits. And that's what really counts."

So, my young friends, when you see people who are not perfect in body or mind, remember the story of Great Eagle and Small One. The Creator loves them each in a special way.

Chapter 6

Great Eagle was a golden eagle. Eagles are birds. They live all over the world.

There are four main kinds of eagles.

- snake eagles
- giant forest eagles
- fish eagles
- booted eagles–golden eagles are in this group

Where Golden Eagles Live

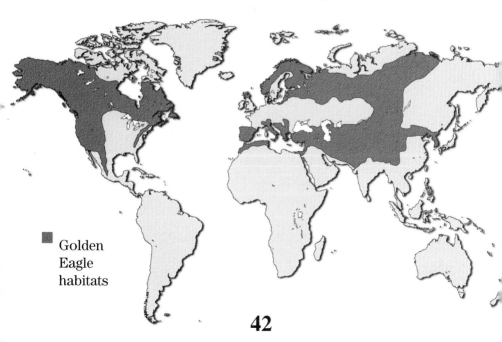

Golden Eagle habitats

Snake Eagles

Snake eagles eat snakes. They crush the snake's head with their claws. They even eat rattlesnakes and cobras! They also eat frogs and lizards.

Giant Forest Eagles

Giant forest eagles live in South America. They eat animals that live in the rain forest. Giant forest eagles love monkey meat.

Fish Eagles

Fish eagles eat fish. They live close to rivers and lakes. The bald eagle is a fish eagle.

Booted Eagles

Booted eagles have long leg feathers. These feathers look like boots. Booted eagles eat many kinds of food. The golden eagle is a booted eagle.

Eagles hatch from eggs. A female eagle often hatches two eggs. Usually only one eaglet lives.

A baby eagle is called an eaglet. It can't hunt. One parent stays in the nest with the baby. The other parent brings food to the nest.

Parents chew the food before they feed it to the baby. That makes it easy for the eaglet to eat.

Corbis

Eaglets stay in the nest. They play with sticks. They grab them with their claws. This helps them learn to hunt.

Eaglets also flap their wings. They sometimes fly a foot or two. Then they fall back into the nest.

After about one month, their baby feathers fall out. They grow flight feathers. Soon they are ready to fly.

Corbis

Eaglets leave the nest when they are three or four months old. They hunt with their parents for a while. Then they learn to hunt alone. Each eagle finds its own place to hunt.

The eagle lives alone until it is four or five years old. Then it finds a mate and builds a nest. Soon there are more eaglets in the world.

Chapter 7

Golden eagles live in many places. There are golden eagles in Russia and China.

These birds also live in the United States. They are found in states like Alaska, California, and New Mexico.

Golden eagles hunt their food. They have very sharp eyes. A golden eagle can see a rabbit half a mile away.

Golden eagles hear well too. Their ears don't stick out like human ears. They are just two holes, one on each side of an eagle's head.

Golden eagles fly very fast. This helps them catch their food.

Golden eagles have large, sharp claws. They use them to grab and hold food.

They use their sharp beaks like knives and forks. Golden eagles love to eat fish, rabbits, and squirrels. They even eat young deer and lamb.

Golden eagles don't like rain. If these birds get too wet, they can't fly. Their feathers become too heavy. So when a storm comes, they hide in a tree or cave.

Golden eagles are protected. It is against the law to hunt them.

But some people hunt them anyway. They worry that eagles will kill their sheep.

This is not true. Golden eagles only hunt what they need to eat. They never kill just for fun.

Golden eagles have other problems too. Some people dump poisons in lakes and rivers where fish live.

Golden eagles eat the fish, and they get sick. Sometimes they die.

Today we have laws against dumping poisons in the water. This helps the eagles. Golden eagles will be here for a long time if we all care for them.